A CHRISTMAS DOLLHOUSE

Richard Rudnicki

NIMBUS
PUBLISHING

To my daughter, Tansy, with love.

A special thanks to Don MacKenzie. This book is inspired by childhood events of Don and his little sister while growing up in depression era Oxford, Nova Scotia. That unexpected gift touched Don deeply, and for many years Don built dollhouses by hand, donating them to charity. He says the best thing is seeing the looks on the faces of the children playing with them.

For all the gracious help given to me in making this book, a deep thank you to Nancy Maxwell, Cheryl Hartland, the Helen Creighton Folklore Society, the Dartmouth Heritage Museum, Alicia Baxter King and her twins, Jodi DeLong, Andrea Hilchie-Pye and her children, Zadie, the Cumberland County Museum and Archives, Kate Broadbelt, the Elizabeth Bishop Society of Nova Scotia, Nelson Hubley, Kelly Rimmington, Dressed in Time, and with much love and appreciation, Susan Tooke.

Nimbus Publishing Limited
3731 Mackintosh St, Halifax, NS B3K 5A5
(902) 455-4286 nimbus.ca

Printed and bound in China

Cover and interior design: Heather Bryan
Author Photo: Susan Tooke

Library and Archives Canada Cataloguing in Publication

Rudnicki, Richard
A Christmas dollhouse / Richard Rudnicki.

ISBN 978-1-55109-868-5

1. Christmas stories, Canadian (English). I. Title.
PS8635.U37C57 2011   jC813'.6   C2011-903923-0

Nimbus Publishing acknowledges the financial support for its publishing activities from the Government of Canada through the Canada Book Fund (CBF) and the Canada Council for the Arts, and from the Province of Nova Scotia through the Department of Communities, Culture and Heritage.

NOVA SCOTIA
Communities, Culture and Heritage

The Canada Council | Le Conseil des Arts
for the Arts | du Canada

It was the last day of school before the Christmas holidays and Dot didn't want to go home. Outside the schoolhouse she looked up at the falling snow. One of her boots had a hole in it. She stuffed it with a bit of paper to keep the cold out.

Miss Teed followed her outside. "Let's go and see the new dollhouse, Dot. I hear it's quite beautiful," she said.

Dot shook her head sadly. She was thinking about her mother, who was very sick. Dot had a lot of chores to do now.

"Come on," said Miss Teed, "it won't take long. I want to see it before Mr. Russell draws for the winner." So Dot hurried after Miss Teed.

When they got to Mr. Russell's drugstore, Dot stopped and stared, pressing her nose against the glass. The dollhouse was perfect, just the sort of house Dot would love to live in. It had wallpaper, tiny rugs, and tiny little paintings. It had a little girl's room, and a nursery for the baby. There was a kitchen with pots and pans, and in the living room was a fireplace with a chimney for old Saint Nick.

Mr. Russell came out of the store and smiled. "Those windows open and close," he said, "and it's got real shingles, but the best part…" He went back inside and plugged a cord into an outlet. The whole dollhouse lit up.

"Lights!" gasped Dot. "The dollhouse has lights!"

Soon there was a crowd squeezing in around Dot and Miss Teed for a closer look.

"For every dollar you spend in my store," said Mr. Russell, "you will get your name in the draw for this dollhouse. I'll draw for the winner on Christmas Eve."

"Hooray!" shouted Dot. Everyone laughed.

When Dot got home, it was snowing hard. Theo and Eddie, the little twins, were wrestling in the snow. Wallis, her older brother, had already done some of her chores.

"Pa got home early," Wallis said. "You'd better get supper on the table."

Dot made a simple meal, and soon it was eaten. Then Pa began to talk.

"We're luckier than some," he said. "There's food on the table, and a roof over our heads." He looked over at Ma. "But we have fallen on hard times, and you children know your Ma is not well. Now I have to get back to cutting those trees in the woods. While I'm away you are going to have to do all the chores around here."

Then he turned to Wallis. "It will be Christmas soon, and I know someone who needs warm gloves." He looked at Dot. "And nobody should have to stuff her boots with papers." To the twins he said, "There will be something for everyone."

That night, Dot cried herself to sleep, worrying about how hard everything was for her family this year, and how poorly her mother was doing.

The next morning she woke up feeling sad. She picked up Buster, the cat, and hugged him. "This is going to be the worst Christmas ever," Dot sniffled.

When she went downstairs, she saw Pa giving a dollar to Wallis.

"Go and see Mr. Russell," Pa said, "and get your Ma's medicine.

"Can I come?" asked Dot. She knew that if they spent a dollar at the drugstore, they could enter the draw for the dollhouse.

At the drugstore window, Dot stopped and showed Wallis the dollhouse. All the lights were on, and the whole house and everything in it was perfect in every way. Dot smiled so hard her cheeks got all bright and shiny.

"Oh," she said, "it's magical. Look, Wallis, it's got real curtains. And there's a kettle on the stove!"

Wallis whistled, and pointed to a picture of a cat hanging on the wall of the baby's room. It looked a lot like Buster. Dot just knew it was a sign that she should have the dollhouse. She pulled Wallis into the drugstore so that they could spend the dollar and get her name in the draw.

Inside the drugstore, they bought the medicine for their mother.

"That will be fifty cents, Wallis," said Mr. Russell.

Dot's smile disappeared. She knew they couldn't spend the rest of the money, not if they didn't have to. She couldn't stop a tear from trickling down her cheek.

Mrs. Pugsley was there too. "Merry Christmas, young lady," she said to Dot. She filled out some tickets for the draw and put them into the ballot box.

Dot and Wallis walked home together.

"Don't be so sad," said Wallis. "You're getting boots for Christmas. You need those more than some old dollhouse."

Dot scrunched her hands up inside her mittens.

The day before Christmas, Dot and Wallis went out to find a Christmas tree. They picked the very best one and happily carried it home.

When they brought it into the parlour, Ma was lying on the sofa.

"Put up the string of popcorn first," she smiled, "then hang the balls. Do the bows last."

The twins helped, hanging decorations on the boughs and eating some of the popcorn. When they were finished, the ornaments on the Christmas tree danced with every breath, and glittered like stars in the sky.

Still, Dot couldn't help looking at the big empty space beneath the tree, and where in other years socks had hung waiting to be filled with oranges and nuts. Most of all, she saw her mother on the sofa, too sick to move. Dot's eyes filled with tears once more, and she went to bed feeling sad.

On Christmas morning, there were four little packages under the tree. There were new, warm boots for Dot, and thick mittens for Wallis. The twins had new wool hats. Dot thought the Christmas tree looked wonderful, and couldn't wait to try out her new boots in the fresh, newly fallen snow outside.

The family gathered close around Ma to share a special gift from Dot for the whole family.

Just then there was a knock at the front door.

Pa opened the door and saw Mr. Russell with a big smile on his face.

"Merry Christmas", said Mr. Russell, and then chuckled.

"Merry Christmas to you too," said Pa, looking confused.

Mr. Russell began to laugh out loud. He looked at everyone and laughed so hard that he couldn't talk. The family looked at him and waited for him to explain why he had come to see them.

"Ha-ha-ha—the dollhouse!" he finally said. "D-D-Dot! She won it!"

Dot looked at Wallis in bewilderment. She knew they hadn't put her name in the draw.

"Every single one," said Mr Russell. "Everybody! They all put Dot's name in the draw!"

He laughed so hard soon everyone else started laughing too.

Pa went outside to help Mr. Russell carry in an enormous box. Dot, with her eyes wide, opened it by the tree. Her heart raced. Right there in front of her was the very dollhouse of her dreams. Dot ran her fingers over the wooden shingles, and opened one of the windows. Then she plugged in the lights. The whole family gasped. They stayed right where they were for just a moment, staring at the little dollhouse so bright and so colourful next to their Christmas tree.

Then there was a stampede. Buster rushed over and sniffed the dollhouse, Wallis opened its door, and one of the twins poked his nose through a window. All the children got down on their tummies and wriggled in for a closer look. Mr. Russell and Pa watched from the doorway, smiling from ear to ear.

And then Dot's mother rose slowly from the sofa and kneeled down beside Dot.

"Show me everything," she said, and watched closely as Dot pointed out every piece of furniture, every dish, and every tiny painting on the walls.

Dot was bubbling over with joy. This was a much better Christmas than she could possibly have imagined. She hugged Buster. She ran and kissed everybody. Then she took Ma's hand in hers and said, "Let's play house!"